2008

For Ian, love always
–E.B.

For Levi, our smallest bun
–J.C.

tiger tales

an imprint of ME Media, LLC
202 Old Ridgefield Road, Wilton, CT 06897
Published in the United States 2008
Originally published in Great Britain 2007
by Little Tiger Press
an imprint of Magi Publications
Text copyright ©2007 Elizabeth Baguley
Illustrations copyright ©2007 Jane Chapman
CIP data is available
Printed in China
ISBN-13: 978-1-58925-074-1
ISBN-10: 1-58925-074-5

A Long Way from Home

by
Elizabeth Baguley

Illustrated by
Jane Chapman

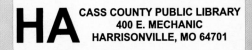
tiger tales

At bedtime in the burrow,
Noah was squished and
squashed by sleepy rabbits.
    "Oh no," he said. "Not again!
Move over, Ella."

Ella squeezed over, folding her arms around Noah like he was her teddy bear.

"Too hot!" muttered Noah.
"Too many rabbits!"
So out into the night he went.

"What are you doing out here, Smallest Bunny?" asked Albatross, swooping down.

"There's no room," snuffled Noah. "And Ella's always squashing me."

"But she's your favorite sister."

"It doesn't keep her from squashing me," said Noah.

To cheer him up, Albatross told Noah about the land of the North Star, where sky and snow went on forever.

"No rabbits there," said Noah, sighing. "I wish I could come with you to the frozen North."

"Hop on then, Smallest Bunny," Albatross said.

Noah squeaked as Albatross
lifted into the air.

Under the moon and over
the wind she flew. As she soared
high, high, higher, Noah held out
his paws like wings.

"I'm flying!" he cried.

"Hold tight! It's the North Star!"
Albatross shouted.

From the North Star came a wild tornado of snow, and before Noah knew it, he had toppled into the storm!

Swept up by the wind, he tumbled and rolled...

down...

and down . . .

to land—*puff!*—
in the snow.

Noah was all alone, and for a moment, he was afraid.
Then he looked around at the empty white space and
hopped with excitement.

"No squish!" he cried. "No squash!"

Noah danced in the snow.
He skated and slid and threw snowballs.
But then—*whoosh!*—he slipped into a
hole and down an ice slide, going faster
and faster until . . .

Noah skidded to a stop.

Oh no! Rabbits everywhere!

As Noah opened his mouth to complain, the other rabbits did, too. But the only sound was Noah's tiny squeak.

"Mirror rabbits!" he gasped
at his reflections in the ice.

Noah was in an ice cave, an ice hall, an ice palace!
It was as big as Big and as quiet as Quiet.
And there was no one there but him.

In the mirror walls, Noah saw himself
as a king, his fluff grand with ice crystals.

Noah made a cool, roomy snow-nest.
"At last, no nest-sharings!" he
pronounced and lay royally down
to sleep.

When Noah woke, his fluff was frozen and he was cold to the bone. Shivering in his lonely bed, he thought about his snuggly sister Ella, squeezed into their nest with all the cozy night-snufflings of his family. Even Noah's tears froze. How he longed to go home!

So out of the palace he fled,
slipping and scrambling up the ice
slide until he came out under the open
sky where the stony moon shone.

"Albatross!" shouted Noah. "Where
are you?"

There was no answer, only the
empty creaking of the ice.

But then Noah heard a feathery whisper on the wind. He looked up and saw wide wings. It was Albatross!

"Smallest Bunny!" she said, relieved. "I've been looking for you everywhere!"

She swung Noah onto her back, and gratefully he nestled into her warm down, thinking only of home.

Back in the nest, Ella rolled over.
Noah was wonderfully squished and
squashed. He was delightfully crumpled and
crammed. He was Ella's teddy bear again.
Noah snuggled into her fluff and with a sigh,
he fell happily asleep.